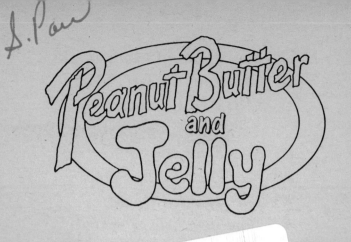

#7 THE FRIENDSHIP TEST

**Look for these and other books
in the PEANUT BUTTER
AND JELLY series:**

#1 *New Friends*
#2 *Peanut and Jilly Forever*
#3 *The Haunted House*
#4 *Trouble at Alcott School*
#5 *Not Starring Jilly!*
#6 *Peanut in Charge*

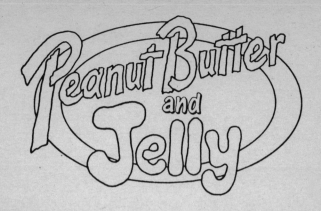

#7 THE FRIENDSHIP TEST

Dorothy Haas

Illustrated by Paul Casale

A
LITTLE APPLE
PAPERBACK

SCHOLASTIC INC.
New York Toronto London Auckland Sydney

ISBN 0-590-43556-6

12 11 10 9 8 7 6 5 4 3 2 1   0 1 2 3 4 5/9

Printed in the U.S.A.   40

First Scholastic printing, July 1990

CHAPTER 1

■▼■▼■▼■▼■▼■▼■▼■▼■

"Miss Kraft is so pretty." Jilly picked up a tray and slid it along the lunchroom tray rail. "I'll be happy if I'm even half as pretty as she is when I grow up."

Peanut — properly known as Polly Butterman, but called Peanut by all her friends — reached into the cooler for milk. One carton or two? Two! She added the second milk to her own tray and moved along, following Jilly. "Being so pretty must mean she's really, really happy. I'll bet nothing ever goes wrong when you're that pretty."

"She looks happy," said Emmy who was

right behind Peanut in the lunch line, "so she must *be* happy. She laughs a lot."

"Don't you just love the way she laughs?" asked Erin. "The way she opens her mouth wide and sort of tosses her head back — I practice doing that every night. Only I haven't got it right yet."

They stopped talking while they filled their trays with hot dogs and french fries and chocolate chip cookies — all except Erin, who had brought her usual egg-ketchup-pickle-relish sandwich from home. She bought only milk and cookies. Making their way among the crowded tables, they found an open place near the windows and slid onto the benches.

"Do you suppose she was pretty when she was our age?" asked Jilly. She bit into her hot dog. Why did the first bite of anything always taste best? She licked her lips.

"She must have been," said Peanut, trying not to eat her hot dog in big gulps. Maggie, her sister, kept telling her she ate too fast. Peanut didn't pay much attention to Maggie. But when her biggest sister Ceci — who was prettier than any TV star — sort of agreed with Maggie, Peanut listened. She was practicing eating slow. "I'll bet," she said, speaking daintily around a teeny-tiny bite, "everything is absolutely perfect when you're pretty. You have pretty clothes and a pretty house and a pretty boyfriend."

"Boyfriends aren't pretty," said Emmy. "Boyfriends are handsome. I wonder," she said thoughtfully, "whatever happened to Mr. X." Emmy had seen Miss Kraft and Mr. X near the apples and oranges at the supermarket. She had called him Mr. X because it sounded glamorous and mysterious. Everybody liked that name.

"He was at the balloon launch," said Jilly.

"And she brought him with her to the haunted house party," said Peanut.

"But I never saw them at the Jewel again," said Emmy. "I always look when we're near the oranges, too. Do you suppose they're still going steady?"

"Were they really going steady?" asked Jilly.

"She never would tell us when we asked her," said Peanut. "She always just laughed."

"He hasn't been around to pick her up after

school in a really long time," said Emmy.

Jilly thought about that for a moment. Then she said, "Neither has anybody else." She eyed her hot dog. It was tasting less and less good.

"Do you suppose maybe she hasn't got any boyfriends at all?" Erin whispered.

They were quiet, considering that terrible idea.

"You've got to have lots of boyfriends," said Peanut. She was an expert on boyfriends from watching Ceci, who had dozens and dozens. "So you can have fun at parties. And so you can pick the right one someday when you want to get married."

"Maybe Miss Kraft is never going to get married," said Emmy.

They stared at each other. Things were looking worse by the moment. Wonderful Miss Kraft, never get married? The thought was bleak, black, awesome.

Jilly considered things. Almost every grown-up she knew was married. Except . . . "My Aunt Barbara isn't married," she said. "She's really pretty. Last summer when she visited us from California I asked her why. Know what she said? She said, 'Oh, do I *have* to?' like maybe she thinks being married isn't so great. She laughed when she said it."

"My Aunt Jean isn't married, either," said Peanut, looking at her hot dog and not taking a bite, and then setting it down on her plate — which was very hard to do. "She's really old — twenty-seven. But she does the most exciting things. She went on a cruise to Mexico last winter. And last summer she went white-water rafting in Idaho."

She took three long breaths before picking up her hot dog again.

"Miss Kraft rode her bike around England last summer," said Emmy. "Imagine riding around a whole country, from sea to sea."

"If she waits a lot longer, maybe she won't find anybody to marry," said Erin. "All the men will be married."

"But if she's happy . . . " said Jilly.

"Maybe we ought to sort of watch her," said Peanut. "If she stops laughing and starts looking sad, maybe we can do something to help her."

"Like what?" demanded Emmy.

Now that was a puzzle. Nobody had any spectacular ideas.

"Well, maybe we can warn her or something," said Peanut. "Maybe I can watch Ceci really closely and pass along some of her secrets to Miss Kraft, and — "

"Girls?"

They looked up, startled.

Miss Kraft was standing behind Peanut. Had she heard them talking about her? They froze.

"I wonder if you'd come back to the room early," said Miss Kraft. "It would help a lot if you'd wipe off the chalkboards before class begins."

She smiled at each of them in turn. She didn't look as though she had heard what they had been saying.

Peanut let out her breath. Jilly's heart stopped pounding. The scared looks faded from Emmy's and Erin's faces. They stepped on each other's words in their relief.

"Yes, ma'am."

"We'll come this very minute."

"I love washing off the boards."

"As soon as I finish this cookie."

"No need to hurry," Miss Kraft said in her easygoing way. "Enjoy your lunch. Just come back to the room ten minutes before the bell rings."

She left them, smiling.

They all felt good. It was super-extra-special to have Alcott School's prettiest teacher stop at their table in the lunchroom to talk with them. And it was going to be fun to be alone with her for a while, without having to share her with all the other kids.

There was no longer time to eat slow. Thank goodness! Peanut took a giant bite of her hot dog. She closed her eyes in bliss as she chewed. Yum-my!

8

CHAPTER
2

Peanut and Jilly wiped off the chalkboard behind Miss Kraft's desk, while Emmy and Erin did the board on the hall side of the classroom. They swooshed their damp sponges over the smeary white rub-outs and made the boards dark green again. The clean boards almost seemed to be asking to have something written on them.

The door into the hall was still closed. Noises came from the outside — yells, whistles, locker doors slamming. But nobody could come into the room until Miss Kraft opened the door. She hummed as she moved around the room,

to and from the supply cabinet, to and from the bookshelves.

Peanut watched her out of the corner of her eye. Would Miss Kraft be humming if she were lonely and unhappy? It didn't seem likely.

Jilly watched her, too. What were all those things Miss Kraft was putting on her desk? There was a battery — no, two batteries . . . a mousetrap . . . the empty fishbowl filled with colored marbles . . . a couple of blocks — the little-kid kind with letters on the sides. . . . And more. What was Miss Kraft getting ready to do this afternoon?

Miss Kraft paused, looking down at the odd array of things. She was smiling at something she was thinking. Would someone smile — and not even at anybody — if they weren't happy?

A loud rap sounded on the glass of the door. They all turned. Ollie Burke's face was close to the glass, his hands cupped around his eyes. He wanted to come in.

Miss Kraft shook her head. Ollie knew the rule. Miss Kraft never let anybody into the classroom until after the afternoon bell rang.

Peanut felt important and proud to be in the room when everyone else was outside. The kids in the hall were probably wondering how come she and the others were in the room. They must be wishing they could be inside, too.

Her hands on her hips, Miss Kraft glanced over at the bookshelves under the windows. She went to the shelves, came back with a handful of nuts, and added them to the clutter on her desk.

Filled with questions, Peanut and Jilly had come to the desk and were looking over the things spread out there.

Jilly could no longer hold in her curiosity. "What's all this stuff for? Are we going to do something with it this afternoon?"

Miss Kraft smiled a secret smile and didn't answer. "Here's a riddle," she said instead. "What kind of nuts does the carpenter squirrel use?"

They stared at her.

"Wall nuts," she said softly. "He uses wall nuts."

The girls groaned and then giggled. Miss Kraft laughed right along with them.

"That's an old chestnut," she said. They didn't catch on. "That means an antique joke."

"I'll bet he takes beach nuts with him when he goes to the lake," said Peanut.

"Does he eat ca-*shew* nuts when he has a cold?" asked Jilly.

"Here's another one," said Miss Kraft. "What state do nuts — "

She was drowned out by the bell. It jangled and went on ringing for the longest time. She went to the door, opened it, and the kids piled into the room.

"How come you guys got to be in here before us?" demanded Ollie.

Emmy pointed at the clean boards. "They were really messy from our math problems."

"Hey, that's a man's job," said Ollie. "Miss Kraft? Miss Kraft? Us boys could have done that better than the girls."

"You," sputtered Emmy, "you . . . "

13

Ollie snorted with laughter. He looked pleased that she was so mad.

"Perhaps next time, Oliver," said Miss Kraft. "People," she called, "people — please take your seats. Let's get started."

"Remember," Peanut murmured to Jilly as they headed toward their desks, "we're going to watch her this afternoon."

"Talk to you after school," Jilly whispered back. Suddenly she thought of something. "Peanut! Let's give her the ladybug test!"

The ladybug test. Peanut's eyes danced. They hadn't done the ladybug test in weeks and weeks. Good things rated ladybugs. The better the thing, the more ladybugs it got. Smile cookies from Maier's Bakery got lots of ladybugs. So did teddy bears and *The Wizard of Oz* movie and Jilly's red-striped tights. Bad things rated spiders. Peanut's tennies, different from everybody else's, got spiders.

"Come to my house," whispered Jilly. "We can see if we noticed the same things."

"After we stop at my house to let Nibbsie out," said Peanut.

The room had quieted down to — as Miss

14

Kraft sometimes said — a "dull roar." Instead of everybody talking to each other, they began asking Miss Kraft questions.

"What's all that stuff on your desk for?" asked Elvis.

"Is it for science?" asked Elena. Then she looked uncertain. "It doesn't really look like science stuff. I mean — marbles?"

"I'd like you to think," said Miss Kraft, "about how things happen, about how one action can cause another action. For example, what happens in baseball?"

"The pitcher throws the ball at the batter," said Nate. "The batter hits it."

"That makes the ball go in the opposite direction," said David.

"Maybe it's a home run," said Courtney. "What happens then is, all the players on base make it home."

"That takes muscle power," said Ollie. "Us men have got more muscle power than girls."

If steam could have come out of Emmy's ears, it would have. Before she could say anything, Miss Kraft said, "The batter makes something happen."

15

"Hockey is like that," said Amy. "The players hit the puck, and the puck slides around on the ice."

"What we're talking about," said Miss Kraft, "is *cause and effect*. One action *causes* something else to happen. Now, I have something in mind."

Everybody leaned forward.

"A friend of mine is studying for an advanced degree and working on a project for the university," Miss Kraft went on. "The project is about how children solve problems. Classes in several cities are taking part in the project. I thought it might be fun for you to be part of it, too. Mr. Granger gave us permission. So if you are interested . . ." She didn't finish the sentence.

The room was still. The project might be fun.

"What we would do," said Miss Kraft, "is work in teams of two. Each team would put a couple of things together so that one moving thing makes something else move. For example, a marble might bump into another marble and the second marble would move.

16

But you would have to figure out how to make that first marble begin to roll."

So that's what the marbles on Miss Kraft's desk meant. The batteries could make a light bulb glow. But the nuts . . . well, maybe a nutcracker could crack them open. But then what would happen?

"We will work on the project this week," said Miss Kraft. "That is, if you are willing. On Friday my friend will visit us to see what we've been up to. Want to try?"

"Neat idea," said David.

"If your friend gets a college degree and we help," said Ollie, "do we get part of the degree, too?"

Everyone turned to stare at him.

"Well, see," said Ollie, "if we're going to work on this, we ought to get something out of it."

Everybody groaned. If that didn't sound just like Ollie!

Miss Kraft didn't get mad. She just smiled at Ollie. "You will have the fun of working on the project," she said softly.

"Listen," said Elvis. "Do we have to do

something that's . . . that's" — he rubbed his forehead, trying to find the right word — "that's, like, for school? Or can we do something that's fun?"

Miss Kraft didn't see anything wrong in doing something for fun.

"Let's go for it, then," said Elvis.

Everyone agreed. "Right." "Okay." "Let's." The voices came from around the room.

"Do we have to use the stuff on your desk? What if we want to use other stuff?" asked Andy.

"The things on my desk are meant to give you ideas," said Miss Kraft. "If you have other thoughts, clear them with me. Now, we'll want to get started right away. We only have until Friday.

"David, will you go to the Learning Center and see what you can find on cause and effect?" She looked around the room. "Jilly, why don't you go with him. The two of you work pretty well together."

Jilly didn't have a chance to talk with Peanut again that afternoon. Not at school, that is.

CHAPTER
3

"Four ladybugs for smiles. She gets four for that." Four ladybugs were the most a person could get for something.

"And four for telling jokes and riddles. What about clothes?"

"We-e-e-ll . . ." Peanut drew out the word, thinking. "I really like almost everything she wears. Except maybe that tan skirt and shirt."

"I think that color is called 'camel,'" said Jilly. "I like it. It's sort of calm when everybody in class is going bananas. What I hate is that black dress."

"I guess she wears that when she's going

someplace special after school," said Peanut. "But most of the time she wears pretty stuff. Three? Three ladybugs for clothes?"

"Three," Jilly agreed. "That means one spider."

"Uh-huh," said Peanut, "for the tan skirt and shirt and the black dress."

They were silent as they drew orange ladybugs and black spiders on their notepads.

They sat hunched over the kitchen table at Jilly's house, eating cookies and rating Miss Kraft on the ladybug scale.

Jilly's mother came into the kitchen as they were drawing. She poured herself a cup of tea and sat down at the table, sipping, watching them. "What's getting the ladybug test today?" she asked, amused. "Spinach? Puce-colored sweaters? I know," she added with a pointed look at Jilly, "cleaning up very untidy bedrooms."

Jilly ignored the bit about untidy bedrooms. "Miss Kraft," she said. "We're giving her the ladybug test."

"But I thought you only gave the ladybug test to things," said Mrs. Matthews. "And I thought you liked Miss Kraft. Why do you need to give her the test?"

"We just love her," said Peanut. "Only we're worried about her."

Mrs. Matthews's left eyebrow lifted, a question without a word spoken.

"We think maybe she hasn't got any boyfriends," Jilly explained. "We're scared she might never get married."

"So we're giving her the ladybug test for getting married things," said Peanut. "If she gets lots of ladybugs it means she will get married even though she doesn't have a boyfriend right now."

Mrs. Matthews laughed.

Why would her mother laugh at something so important? Jilly wondered. She was never going to understand grown-ups.

"And how many ladybugs did she get?" asked Mrs. Matthews. "And how many spiders?"

Peanut and Jilly counted.

"Twenty-six ladybugs," said Peanut. "One spider."

"Twenty-nine ladybugs," said Jilly. "One

spider." She leaned over to look at Peanut's paper. "Maybe you didn't count right."

"Maybe *you* counted wrong," said Peanut.

Hastily they began a recount.

"You know," said Mrs. Matthews, taking a cookie from Jilly's plate, "I don't think there's the least danger whatsoever of Miss Kraft not getting married." She nibbled at the cookie. "She's so full of fun."

After a quiet moment she said, "Funny that you girls should be worrying about that."

Peanut and Jilly looked up from their counting.

"Twenty-seven," said Jilly, "and still only one spider."

"Me, too," said Peanut. "Twenty-seven ladybugs."

"So many ladybugs has to mean she'll get married," said Jilly.

"Time was," said Mrs. Matthews, "when girls absolutely had to be married. It was often a case of get married or starve. There weren't many kinds of work they could do to make a living. Today women run stores and offices and are doctors and lawyers and police officers and — oh, lots of things. Just a hundred years ago that wasn't true."

Just a hundred years ago? That sounded like dinosaur times to Jilly, and she said as much.

"Your very own great-grandmothers lived in those days," said Mrs. Matthews. "Be glad you girls didn't. You will grow up to be . . . well . . . whatever you like."

A sound came from the front of the house. The front door had opened.

"Daddy?" came a call. It was Jackie, Jilly's little brother, home from his sitter's house. "I'm home."

"Out here in the kitchen, sweetie," called Mrs. Matthews. "Mrs. Potter? Are you there? Want to join me in a cup of tea?"

"Not today, thanks," called Mrs. Potter. "I have to get to the post office before five. I'll be on my way."

The door in the distance slammed, and Jackie came running into the kitchen. He leaped onto his mother's lap. "Where's Daddy? How come you're home from school so soon? Did Jason

24

say any more words today? Can I have some hot chocolate? Mrs. Potter and I had the best time today. We went to story hour at the library."

Mrs. Matthews kissed him and gave him a big hug that ended in a tickle. He shrieked with laughter. "Daddy's downtown in the Loop. He had to deliver some artwork," she said. "I'm here because he isn't. No, Jason didn't say anything today. Now climb down, and I'll make you some hot chocolate."

Jackie slid off her lap, looking around. "Where's Bonkers? I have to say hello to her. Bonkers? Bonkers, where are you?" He ran to look for his cat. "Bonkers? Bonkers?" His voice echoed through the house. "Listen, Bonk — you can't hide from me."

"How can one little boy make so much noise?" sighed Mrs. Matthews, getting up and going to the pantry to get the cocoa.

"Who's Jason?" asked Peanut.

"A kid in Mom's class," Jilly explained. "He hardly ever talks. Except every now and then he surprises her and says some words. Mom feels really great when he does."

25

"Why doesn't he talk?" asked Peanut. How could a person stand not talking!

"He's . . . he's . . . " Jilly didn't know why. "He's handicapped, is all. That's why he's in Mom's class. I bet she'll get him to talk all the time pretty soon." She picked up a cookie, looked at it, and put it back on her plate. She was full.

Peanut picked up a cookie and bit it in half. She was always hungry! "These are the greatest," she said through a mouthful of crumbs. "I wish Miss Kraft lived near school. We could watch her house, and then we'd know for sure about boyfriends."

"She lives way out on Golf Road," said Jilly. "So we can't watch her house. How can we worry right about her if we can't see what she does after school?"

The problem didn't seem to have any answer.

"I'm glad we gave her the test." Jilly folded her pages neatly. "It will be kind of comforting to look at when we worry about her."

CHAPTER
4

The teams were scattered around the class-room. The air hummed with talk as they planned their projects.

"The boat's got to float." That was Erin. She was working with Ollie. "How'll we get it to float?"

"Water, Dumbo," said Ollie. "What else makes boats float? Miss Kraft? Miss Kraft? It's okay to use water in the project, isn't it?"

Nate and Andy were a team. They wanted to do something with a spaceship.

"Maybe we could use a rubber band to get it moving." Nate liked that idea. "You know — snap it."

"How about we just blow on it?" asked Andy.

"But could we blow hard enough?" asked Nate. "And hey — is there wind on the moon?"

Andy wasn't sure.

Jilly and David were curled up in a corner at the back of the room.

"Listen," said David, "how about using one of my little cars?"

"How will we make it start to roll?" asked Jilly.

"Down a ramp?" asked David.

That sounded hard. "Can we make one?" asked Jilly.

"Nothing to it," said David. "Just a piece of wood leaning against one of the blocks." He had a new thought. "Could you draw a man with a flag to start the race?"

Jilly didn't think that would be hard. "I can put him on cardboard so we can make him stand up."

Nearby, Peanut and Elvis were sitting with their backs against the supply cabinet.

"It sure would be a hoot to let a bunch of balloons go," said Elvis.

"That means they would have to have he-

lium in them," said Peanut. "How would we do that?"

"I saw a sign in Chandler's window," said Elvis. "They fill balloons. I guess you've got to buy the balloons from them," he added.

Imagine setting a whole bunch of balloons free to float around the room! Peanut loved the idea. "We've got to figure out how to let them go free."

"Lots of stuff should happen when we do," said Elvis. "Like a bell ringing and a light flashing and a siren going off."

"Jilly's little brother showed me one of his toys yesterday," said Peanut. "It's really funny. Maybe he'll lend it to me. It moos."

Elvis looked gleeful. "What a blast!"

Miss Kraft clapped her hands. "You've had your thinking time, people. Now it's get-down-to-business time. Will you put in a little work on your own at home tonight?"

Everybody groaned. The loudest groan came from Ollie. "Homework! We're getting killed dead with homework."

Miss Kraft just laughed at him.

Peanut's and Jilly's eyes met. Miss Kraft laughed even when someone was being a pain.

Erin noticed, too. Watching Miss Kraft closely, she tossed her head back. But she didn't laugh.

"Well, Oliver," said Miss Kraft, "I suppose if you want to drop out of the project and miss all the fun. . . . "

Ollie slid down in his seat and hunched his shoulders. Of course he didn't want to miss out on all the fun!

"Most of you need to put things together," Miss Kraft went on. "It might be simpler to do that at home where you have screwdrivers and glue and whatever."

"Friday," said Elena. "That's when your friend is coming to see what we do. That's just the day after tomorrow."

"Yes," said Miss Kraft. "You can see we don't have a lot of time. Teams, suppose you sit down and draw a picture of exactly what you plan on doing. Come to my desk to show me when you finish."

Jilly did the drawing. David made suggestions. The picture showed the car going down a slanted piece of wood. A man stood at the top of the ramp holding a flag. The car was going to bump a marble and make it roll. The plan looked like a pretty good one.

"You know," said David, "instead of the man being cardboard, suppose I make him out of wood. I can use my dad's saw to cut him out, and you can paint him tomorrow while I put the ramp together."

"You're doing most of the work," said Jilly. "I'm just painting. That's not fair."

"Can you cut out the man?" asked David. "Can you build the ramp?"

Jilly had to admit she couldn't.

"Well, I can't draw or paint," said David. "I mean I can, but not as good as you do."

Put that way, things did seem fair.

Elvis drew the picture of the balloon plan. He made the balloons red and purple and wrote words all around them like *pow!* and *bam!*

"If we have all those words," Peanut pointed out, "maybe we'd better think of a way to pop some of the balloons."

Elvis smacked his forehead with his hand. "Wow! Why didn't I think of that?"

"Because you're not as smart as I am," Peanut said pertly, laughing.

"Sez who?" said Elvis. But he giggled. Elvis giggled at everything.

Before they finished the drawing, they thought they had a way — maybe, just maybe — to make some of the balloons explode.

After school, Peanut and Jilly and Emmy and Erin went to 31 Flavors. They sat on the chairs in the window and licked their ice-cream cones and talked about the project.

"I wish Miss Kraft would let best friends work together," Erin said wistfully.

"David is making the stuff we need," said Jilly, "and I'm painting it. I can't build and he can't paint. Maybe you and Ollie do different things, too."

Emmy had been quiet, thinking. "I wonder if Miss Kraft's friend will be pretty."

"Remember Miss Maya?" said Jilly. "She was super-gorgeous." Miss Maya had directed their play.

"She is so dark," said Peanut, "and Miss Kraft is so fair. Maybe this friend will have red hair."

"And green eyes," said Erin. "Wow!"

Emmy suddenly remembered something. "I saw you watching Miss Kraft this afternoon. You both saw the same thing. I know, because you looked at each other."

Peanut and Jilly looked at each other now, remembering how Miss Kraft had laughed when Ollie was being pesky.

"There! You're doing it again," said Emmy. "Do you know something we don't know? Tell! Tell!"

Without saying a word to each other, Peanut and Jilly knew it was okay to tell Emmy and Erin. Best friends do that sometimes — each knowing what the other is thinking without saying one single word.

"Well, see," said Peanut, licking her cone into a point at the top, "we're watching her like crazy because we gave her the ladybug test."

"And we wanted to see if we missed anything," said Jilly.

Emmy and Erin forgot to eat. Melted ice cream ran down the cones and onto their fingers. They knew all about ladybug tests. They spoke at the same time. "Did she get lots of ladybugs?" "What things did she get ladybugs for?"

"Smiling and laughing," said Jilly. "And wearing pretty clothes."

Erin looked down at her pink sweater. "Are my clothes pretty? Would I pass the ladybug test?"

"Did you guys pass the test?" asked Emmy.

Peanut and Jilly stared at her. Why, they hadn't even thought of giving the test to themselves!

"The test was for grown-ups," said Peanut, "not for kids. It was to see if Miss Kraft would get lots of ladybugs, and that would mean she's going to get married someday. She did. And now we can stop worrying about her."

"And anyway," said Jilly, thinking about how she and Peanut had given the test to Miss Kraft, "we couldn't give the test to ourselves. So we don't know if we'd pass it."

"You changed the test from one for things

to one for people," said Erin. "I don't see why you can't change it again and make it a test for kids."

"Like," said Emmy, "a most popular person test. I mean, if you're not popular now, maybe you will be someday — if you get lots of ladybugs."

"And then you can stop worrying about when you get to high school," said Erin.

Peanut and Jilly turned to each other. It would be nice to know that, about being popular, before they grew up.

What a terrific idea!

"Let's!" said Peanut.

"Oh, let's!" said Jilly.

They slurped down the rest of their ice cream and licked their sticky fingers and went to Jilly's house to work on another kind of ladybug test.

CHAPTER
5

"We can use the question about smiling and laughing," said Jilly. "That's important no matter how old a person is."

"And the ones about being pretty and wearing pretty clothes and telling jokes and riddles," said Peanut.

"But not" — Jilly shook her head — "the one about makeup."

"We'll have to make up some questions just for kids," said Peanut.

Thinking up new questions took lots of time. Peanut and Jilly chewed on their pencils and thought and talked in low voices while Emmy and Erin sat on the hall steps playing with Jilly's cat, Bumptious.

Slowly the questions sorted themselves out. There was one about being able to keep secrets and another about playing sports. Peanut and Jilly were especially pleased with the one about knowing how to be a true friend.

"Done!" Peanut said at last.

"They're pretty good," said Jilly.

Grinning at each other, they called Emmy and Erin in from the hall and explained again how things worked, just in case they didn't remember.

"When you're finished, you add up all the ladybugs and spiders."

"The more ladybugs you get, the more certain you are to be a popular person."

"This test can be really helpful," said Peanut. "If you get lots of spiders, you'll know what things you've got to get better at."

"What a super test," sighed Erin. "I've never heard of anything like this. I mean, a ladybug test for popularity."

"Erin and I will have to talk about you,"

said Emmy, eyeing Peanut and Jilly, "so we'd better go to my house."

"We'll call you up and tell you about your ladybugs as soon as we finish," said Erin. "And then you can tell us about ours."

"But we can't do that," said Jilly. "Our phone is off-limits this week. My dad's doing a big job for Marshall Field's. Jerry and I can't use the phone."

"I can't use our phone tonight, either." Peanut made a face. "Except for three-minute calls. Ceci got into a state last night when I talked to Jilly for a half hour. She was hoping for a call from a boy."

Erin sighed. "Who knows? I might just die in my sleep tonight. Then I'll never know how many ladybugs I got."

"Let's get to school early tomorrow morning," said Peanut. "We can meet at the tetherball pole at eight-fifteen."

"Don't be late," Erin wailed. "I don't think I can stand to wait."

Emmy and Erin headed for home, their heads close together as they looked over the list of questions.

Jilly watched them out the front window. "I wonder if they're talking about you or about me?" She wasn't sure she liked being talked about.

"Me," said Peanut, grinning. "They're telling each other how great I am."

They went upstairs to Jilly's room and curled up with the stuffed animals on the beds. Except that one of the animals wasn't stuffed. Bumptious came quietly into the room, circled it on silent paws, and jumped up next to Jilly. She smoothed the silky gray fur.

"I wish I could bring Nibbsie here with me," said Peanut. She missed Nibbsie when she was at Jilly's house and saw her stroking Bumptious.

"It's too bad they hate each other," said Jilly. She picked up Bumptious and looked her right in the eye. "Bumpy, you get sixteen spiders for hating Nibbsie."

Peanut laughed. "I don't think the ladybug test works for cats and dogs. I mean, it's sort of natural for dogs and cats not to like each other."

"They don't know what they're missing," said Jilly.

And then they got down to work rating Emmy and Erin.

Emmy and Erin were waiting for them when they got to school the next morning.

"Tell!" Erin commanded, hopping up and down. "Oh, tell! I could hardly sleep all night wondering."

"Did we do okay?" asked Emmy. She sounded excited — and worried.

Peanut and Jilly were wondering about their own scores. But they took pity on Erin because she fussed and fretted about things. She really suffered more than anybody they knew.

"Twenty-four ladybugs, Erin," said Jilly. "You got twenty-four."

Erin smiled an uncertain smile. "But that means I got four spiders."

"Well, you can't be perfect," Peanut said matter-of-factly. "Miss Kraft is just about perfect, and she only got twenty-seven."

"How about me?" demanded Emmy.

"Twenty-four, too," said Peanut.

Emmy looked pleased. "We match!"

"Not exactly," said Jilly. "You got spiders for different things."

"Emmy," said Peanut, "you got two ladybugs for wearing nail polish — "

"My mother won't let me wear nail polish," moaned Erin.

"But you got two spiders for biting your nails," Peanut went on.

Emmy sighed. "That's why I get to wear the nail polish — to remind me not to chew on my nails. Only I always forget. What are the other two spiders for?"

"For making us guess what's on your mind and not even giving us a hint when you know something," said Jilly.

"But that's fun," said Emmy, her eyes sparkling. "Isn't it?"

"No . . . it . . . is . . . not!" Peanut and Jilly said together.

Erin did some more hopping around. "You haven't told me. What did I get spiders for?"

"For not keeping secrets," said Jilly. "You always forget and tell when you get excited. Two spiders."

"Oh, that," said Erin. "That's not important."

"It is, too!" they yelled at her.

Erin looked sheepish. "Okay. I'll try to get
better. What else?"

"Losing things," said Peanut. "You lose more
things than any kid in class. Now you tell us.
How did we do?"

"You got twenty-four ladybugs each," said
Erin. "We're alike, the four of us."

"What did we get spiders for?" asked Jilly.
Her stomach scrunched up in her middle. She
wasn't sure she wanted to know!

Their heads together, Emmy and Erin bent
over their score sheets. They looked up laughing. "Isn't this funny?" said Erin. "You got
them sort of for the same thing, only different."

If that wasn't just like Erin! She was never
very clear about things. How could they be
the same and different? Jilly rolled her eyes
at Peanut.

Emmy explained. "Well, see, Jilly got two
spiders for sometimes not talking much. Like
when she gets all quiet."

That again. Jilly hated when people noticed

her quietness. She didn't know what to do about it.

"Peanut," said Emmy, "you got two spiders for sometimes talking too much. Sometimes you're never quiet."

Peanut howled with laughter. After a moment Jilly joined in. They leaned against each other gasping for breath because they were alike but different about talking.

"You both got four ladybugs for pretty smiles and laughing a lot," said Erin. "But you each got spiders for taking a dare too fast."

"Like that time," said Emmy, "when you climbed to the top of the garage roof on the other side of the schoolyard fence because Ollie said girls couldn't do that. And Mr. Larson had to bring a ladder from the furnace room so you could get down."

Emmy was right. They should not have taken that dare — as Mr. Granger, Alcott's principal, had pointed out when they had to go to his office.

Ollie had laughed for days and days, saying that they had proved he was right.

"What are you all talking about?" Courtney

had joined them just in time to hear about ladders and furnace rooms.

"Is something good going on?" asked Carrie who was with Courtney.

The schoolyard was filling up. Elena and Gina came along while Emmy and Erin were explaining Peanut and Jilly's ladybug scores. They were closely followed by the rest of the girls.

"So now we know what things we've got to work on," said Erin.

"But you're all pretty sure to be popular," said Elena. "How neat! Can I take that test? I'd like to know about it, too."

"So would I," said Courtney.

By the time the bell rang, all the girls were eager to take the ladybug test.

What fun! It was the best thing Peanut and Jilly had thought up in ages.

CHAPTER
6

Nobody could take the ladybug test during class time, of course. But everyone needed the questions. Jilly slipped them to Courtney, who copied them and passed them along to Allison. She wrote them down and gave them to Carrie . . . who passed them to Beth . . . who passed them to Gina. It took almost the whole morning to get the questions to everybody.

When Courtney went up and down the rows passing out papers for Miss Kraft, she murmured "ladybug test" to the girls. The girls couldn't help grinning and giving each other knowing looks.

When Rachel picked up the papers, she whispered "ladybug test," too. The girls wiggled around in their seats and thought the day would never end. They talked about the test at recess and in the lunchroom and during art class. That's where Elvis and Ollie heard them.

"What's the ladybug test?" asked Ollie.

"Is it a test Miss Kraft is going to give us?" asked Elvis.

Boys take the test? Peanut and Jilly nearly fell apart laughing.

"Unh-uh," said Jilly when she caught her breath. "It's just something us girls are doing."

"You wouldn't like it," Peanut assured them. "I give you my word — you would not like this test."

"How can we know if you don't tell us?" asked Ollie. His lip stuck out. He was annoyed with the girls.

But no matter how hard he and Elvis begged, Peanut and Jilly would not tell them what they wanted to know.

The ladybug test was forgotten for a while

in the afternoon when they worked on their projects. They had to get all the kinks ironed out today. Tomorrow was Project Day when Miss Kraft's friend would come to look at them.

As he had promised, David had brought the wooden cutout of a man. The arm on one side moved — he had put it on with wire. "I had a flag in his hand," he told Jilly, "but the saw slipped and cut it off."

"That won't be hard to fix," said Jilly. "I'll make one out of paper and tape it to his arm. I wonder," she said, thinking. "Can we fix it so his arm is down with the car leaning against it? When his arm goes up — "

"The car moves!" said David, excited. "I think I know how to make that happen."

While David worked on his idea, Jilly got out her paints. She knew what she was going to do. She would draw the man's face with pen and ink. He would have white pants and a blue sweater. The flag would be red, white, and blue. Maybe it would have a star on it.

Peanut and Elvis were working on their balloon project, only half listening to each

49

other as they talked. Elvis was most interested in how the balloons could be made to burst. Peanut was more interested in the noises that would be a fun part of the balloon lift-off.

"Look." She held up a small glass bell. "This is from my sister's bell collection. She bought it when she went to the Dells. She'll murder me if she notices I borrowed it without asking. But I couldn't ask her — she had left for school when I thought about the bell. We can tie it to one of the balloon strings. It will ring when the balloon goes up."

"Pow!" said Elvis. "Ka-bam! Everybody's going to dive under their desks when the balloons bust. They'll think bombs are going off."

"Listen to this," said Peanut. She held out a small round box with a picture of a cow on it. She turned the box over.

MOOOOO-OOOOO-OOOOO. A mournful sound came from the box.

Everybody in the room turned. Where had that cow sound come from?

Elvis exploded into giggles. Hastily Peanut

covered the moo-toy. "I promised Jilly's little brother I'd take good care of this," she said.

Elvis held out a handful of straight pins. "I took these out of some cloth my mom left lying on the table. All we've got to do is push them through Scotch tape, stick the tape on one of the balloons, and we'll have — Porcupine Balloon, the Great Popper. When the other balloons bump him, they'll bust."

"But not all at once," said Peanut. "We don't want them to explode all at the same time."

"We don't?" Clearly Elvis thought it would be super if the balloons all exploded in one glorious popping.

"We're spending our whole week's allowance on the balloons," said Peanut. "Some of them should float around for a while."

Elvis sighed. "You're spoiling things."

"Come on, Elv," said Peanut, "get serious. We've still got to figure out how to set the balloons loose."

They sat there frowning at each other. Scissors? Tie the balloons to a chair and cut them loose? There had to be a better way. But they didn't think of anything. Maybe if they thought about it overnight. Well, they had *better* think of something tonight!

Peanut dug the rest of her allowance out of her jeans. "I wonder how many balloons this will buy."

Elvis pocketed the money. "A lot, I think, when it gets added to mine. I'll get my dad to take me to Chandler's tonight. I'll buy as many balloons as we've got money for."

The girls were waiting, bouncing in their seats, when the bell finally rang. They beat the boys to the door.

Miss Kraft watched them scramble out of the room, a thoughtful look on her face. The girls certainly were excited about something.

Outdoors, on the steps, everybody clustered around Peanut and Jilly.

"You have to work in teams to take the test," Jilly explained.

Quickly the girls sorted themselves into pairs. Courtney and Elena teamed up with Allison and Beth, and Rachel and Carrie with April and Gina.

Nearby, Ollie and Elvis were fooling around

with a basketball, keeping an eye on the girls. At last they could no longer hold down their curiosity. They ambled toward the group on the steps.

"Need a couple of strong men for your lady-bug test?" asked Ollie.

"Strong, *smart* men?" said Elvis.

The girls burst into giggles. How many ladybugs would Ollie and Elvis get?

Ollie's ears turned purple. Elvis looked as though people were keeping a good joke from him, and he wanted to hear it, too.

"You know, Oll," Jilly said mildly, "I don't think you really want to take this test."

Ollie's jaw stuck out. "How do you know? All you've got to do is tell us about it, and we'll decide."

But Peanut and Jilly didn't want to tell Ollie. Ollie made fun of everything they did.

"Us guys can pass any test you take and make you look like bubbleheads in the bargain," said Ollie. "Just let us at that test."

That did it! Ollie had gone too far. Peanut and Jilly didn't even have to talk about it.

"Sure, you can take the test, Ollie," Peanut

said softly, sweetly — too sweetly. "If you really want to."

The other girls had grown quiet, listening. Something silly and great was happening here!

"You bet we want to," said Ollie. "What do we do?"

"Not a single thing," said Peanut. "Jilly and I will rate you. Meet us here tomorrow before school, and we'll give you your ladybug scores."

"Are ladybugs the prize?" asked Ollie.

"You can't find ladybugs at this time of year," said Elvis. "Are you gonna get them at the pet shop? Do you give them out in jars?"

"You'll find out tomorrow," said Peanut, doing her best not to look as though she had a secret.

The girls all headed for home, eager to get on with their own ladybug tests. They could barely wait for morning and their ladybug scores.

"Girls!" said Ollie, watching them go.

"Were they maybe laughing in a kind of funny way?" asked Elvis as he dribbled the basketball toward the basketball hoop.

"That's just because they're weird," said Ollie, catching up with him. He got the basketball away from Elvis and tossed it up toward the hoop. He almost made the basket, too.

CHAPTER 7

Peanut and Jilly took Nibbsie to the park for a run. He scampered around, chasing the stick they tossed for him while they talked about Ollie and Elvis.

"We've got to give Elvis four ladybugs for telling jokes. He makes us all laugh. Wouldn't our class be dull without Elvis?"

"Some of the jokes are really cornball, though."

"Even if they make you groan, they're funny. It's the way he tells them."

"Okay. Four for jokes. But Ollie sure doesn't get four ladybugs for jokes. I've never heard him tell a really funny one. What he thinks is funny is calling somebody muttonhead or something."

"But he laughs at jokes. I mean, I think he does."

But they couldn't exactly remember seeing Ollie laugh at a joke.

Well, make it three spiders and one ladybug. No — better make it two of each. Because he did *try* to be funny.

"What about jewelry? Can we use that question? Maybe it wouldn't be fair — boys don't wear jewelry."

"We'd better skip that one. We'll use six questions instead of seven. We can use the one about pretty clothes, though."

"*Pretty* is the wrong word for boys. Okay, clothes — that's better. I really like Ollie's Cubs jacket. I like his yellow sweater, too."

"Elvis has that Bulls sweatshirt. I wish I had one like it."

"Did you ever see that tie thing Elvis wears when he's dressed up? It's braided leather and it closes with a piece of turquoise."

Nibbsie came running. He dropped the stick and rolled on the grass at their feet.

Peanut picked up the stick and threw it. The fluffy little dog raced away. "Will you make Ollie's ladybug score sheet? I'll make Elvis's because we're working together on the project."

Nibbsie was back, yipping. Peanut gathered him up in a big hug. "I haven't been paying enough attention to you, Nibbs, have I? I'll make it up to you tonight. Okay?"

Nibbsie licked her nose.

Jilly stuffed her hands into her pockets to warm them up. "I'll come to your house tomorrow morning. Early. I can hardly wait to get to school and see how well everybody did on their ladybug tests."

"This is the most fun thing we've done in a long time."

Fun! Fun! Fun!

Never in a million years could they have guessed what would be waiting for them when they got to school the next morning.

* * *

They were still half a block away from school when Peanut said, "Elvis is there already. I can see balloons."

"So are the girls," said Jilly, peering around and past all the kids racing around the schoolyard.

They quickened their steps and rounded the fence, heading for the tetherball pole.

"Hi!" called Jilly as they neared the group. "How'd you all do on the ladybug test?"

She was met with silence.

Courtney didn't look up from the circle she was tracing with the toe of her shoe.

Elena did look up. There were tears in her dark eyes.

Rachel sniffed. Carrie bit her lip. April was biting her nails — and she wasn't a nail biter. Gina . . . Allison . . . Beth — they all stared at Peanut and Jilly without speaking. There wasn't a smile among them. Not even Elvis, always-good-for-a-giggle Elvis, was smiling. He stood under a cluster of bobbing balloons looking glum.

Ollie, his hands on his hips, glared at Peanut and Jilly. "A dumb popular person test!"

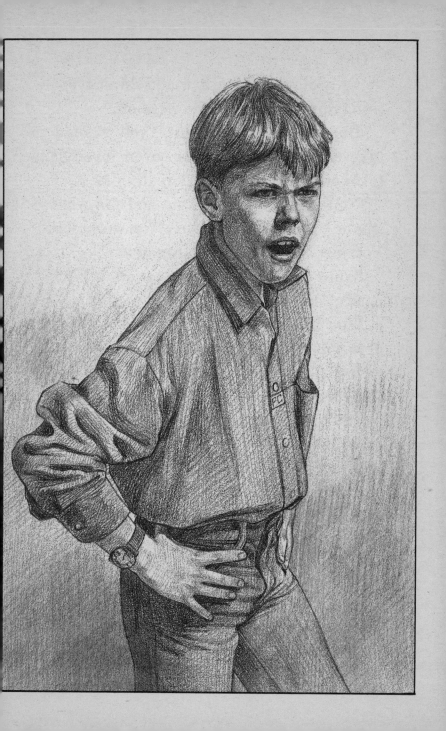

Oh!

"Only dumbhead girls would think of something dumb like that," he went on.

"But Ollie," said Peanut, "you wanted to take the test. You said so, even when Jilly told you that you wouldn't really like it."

"You should've told Elvis and me what it was all about," said Ollie. "We wuz robbed. You just wanted to make fun of us."

"Well, you shouldn't have called us bubbleheads," said Peanut.

"You know, it's really kind of fun knowing how many ladybugs you got," said Jilly. "We gave you ladybugs for your clothes, like your Cubs jacket, and — and — "

At the words "your clothes," tears spilled down Elena's cheeks.

"You're a pair of meatheads," said Ollie. "Come on, Elv — let's go shoot some baskets."

Elvis trailed away after Ollie, hanging onto the balloons, looking as though he wondered how he could shoot baskets and hang onto the balloons at the same time.

"But Ollie," Peanut called, "don't you even

want to know what your ladybug score was? It was pretty good."

He didn't turn around or answer.

Peanut watched the boys go. Then she thought of something. "Hey — who told Ollie what the ladybug test was for?"

"I did," April admitted after an uncomfortable minute. "But he made me. I mean, I only told because he said we were stupid, and he was smarter than ten of us put together."

So that was it. Ollie had found out what the test meant before he had a chance to hear his score. Maybe he wouldn't have been so mad if he had found out his score before he found out what the test was all about.

"He *wanted* to take the test," Peanut murmured to Jilly. All the same, she felt funny — like there were spiders crawling around in her middle. Maybe it hadn't been fair to take Ollie at his word when she sort of guessed he wouldn't like the test. . . .

Jilly looked around the group of unhappy girls. She kind of understood about Ollie. But what was wrong with the girls? Why did they all look so sad? She dug a crumpled piece of Kleenex out of her pocket and went to Elena. "Want this?" she asked.

Elena took it and mopped at her eyes.

"What's wrong?" Jilly asked. "Why are you crying?"

"Because — " Elena hiccuped. "Because," she went on in a shaky voice, "I got a really low ladybug score because my clothes aren't pretty and now I'm never going to be a popular person."

"But your clothes *are* pretty," said Jilly. "I love your pink shirt and the scarf for your hair. Pink is your color. And the Mexican skirt and blouse you wore when you danced for the PTA meeting were so pretty."

"You're the only girl in class with pierced ears," said Peanut. "I love your gold earrings."

"I'd give anything if I could have my ears pierced," said Jilly. She glanced around the group. Why was everybody else so gloomy?

Slowly the answers came out.

"My teeth are crooked."

"I have to wear these ugly glasses."

"My hair is too curly."

"My hair is too straight. I can't make it curl."

"They said I laugh funny."

"They said I'm a show-off about my new clothes."

Too skinny. Too fat. Terrible at sports. Nose too big. Nose too small. Mouth too big. Mouth too small. Too many freckles —

And the ladybug scores — oh, those were simply terrible.

"I only got twelve ladybugs."

"Me — I only got eight."

Seven. Fourteen. Eleven. Nine. The dreadful ladybug scores were interrupted by the bell.

The girls filled into school, into class, quietly. Too quietly.

Peanut and Jilly stared at each other across the rows of desks. What had gone wrong? The ladybug test was supposed to be fun for everybody. But this morning everybody looked as though the world was going to come to an end at exactly nine-oh-two.

Oh, what had they done!

CHAPTER
8

The last bell rang and Miss Kraft closed the door. She looked around the strangely still room, not saying anything for a moment. "My goodness," she said softly, almost to herself, "did somebody turn off the bubble machine?"

Some of the boys laughed. But Ollie didn't. Neither did Elvis.

"Did you all forget to take your vitamin pills this morning?"

Wan smiles appeared on a few of the girls' faces.

"Have you forgotten that today is Project Day? I see you've brought your balloons, Elvis.

66

I hope the rest of you remembered to bring the things you need."

There was a quiet stir as everybody began to come to life.

"We want to be ready by ten o'clock," said Miss Kraft. "Why don't we get right down to business? Ladies and gentlemen — start your engines."

Normally there would have been a general hoopla at those words, the ones starters say at automobile races. Today was different. Quietly partners got together and began setting up their projects.

"Did you bring the flagman?" David asked Jilly.

Jilly set him on the bookshelf.

David turned him, looking at him from all sides. "Great. Just great. And I brought these." He dug into his pockets and spilled dominoes onto the bookshelf.

"What are those for?" asked Jilly.

"I thought about them last night," said David. "They'll make the project go on longer. You'll see in a second."

"We'd better do a test," said Jilly. "To see if

everything happens the way we think it's going to."

The ladybug test and all the strangeness of the last hour faded as everybody worked on their projects.

Miss Kraft looked around. Her eyes settled on Elena, on Elena's red eyes. Going to her, she spoke softly. Elena shook her head. Miss Kraft hugged her and moved on.

"Look, Elvis," said Peanut as they tied the crystal bell to one of the balloon strings. "I'm really sorry. We didn't mean to make you mad. You can pop all the balloons if that'll make you feel better."

It didn't take a whole lot to make Elvis feel better, not ever. He grinned. "You mean it? All *right!*"

It was the least Peanut could do to make things up to him. "And listen," she added, "did I ever tell you I really, really like your Bulls sweatshirt?"

Elvis looked down at the sweatshirt and patted his chest. "I hope I grow up to be tall. Maybe I'll get to play basketball with the Bulls."

Peanut began to feel better. But she was going to have to make it up to Ollie, too. And the girls — what was she going to do about them?

"If you want to get the books," she said to Elvis, "I'll start stacking them on the strings to hold the balloons down."

Chatter in the room rose to something like the usual quiet roar. It all jumbled together.

"Ouch! Did you have to snap that rubber band at me? Do you know what that *causes* me to do? It *causes* me to snap one back at you. War! The great rubber band war!"

"But we've got to keep the Porcupine Balloon away from the others till we set them loose."

"My brother showed me how to cut a hole in the tin can. When we pull out the plug, the marbles are gonna fall out of it."

"Hey! We just thought of a way to sort of join our project to yours. Our marble can drop into your tin can full of marbles."

Everybody was so busy that they didn't notice the door open and someone come into the room.

"People?" Miss Kraft clapped her hands. "Are you all set up?"

"Wait. Oh, wait!"

"Just another minute. Our mousetrap won't stay open."

"We're almost ready over here."

Quiet settled over the room as everybody realized that a stranger was standing beside Miss Kraft. Well — not quite a stranger. . . .

"Mr. X!" gasped Peanut.

"What's he doing here?" breathed Jilly.

"What are you guys talking about?" asked Elvis.

"He's been away at college!" said Peanut, suddenly understanding. "That's why we haven't seen him around!"

"I told you Mr. Holliday would be here this morning to see what we've done with our cause-and-effect projects," said Miss Kraft.

Erin moved close to Jilly, her eyes on the tall man. "I thought Miss Kraft's friend was a lady," she hissed.

"She never said her friend was a lady," whispered Jilly. "We just thought so. All she

said was her 'friend.' " But she was every bit as surprised as Erin.

Mr. Holliday smiled. There were crinkles around his eyes, as though he laughed a lot. "Hi, cohorts," he said. "Cohorts — that means my partners in crime. Want to let me see what you've been doing?"

He moved around the room looking at projects.

Nate and Andy didn't blow on their spaceship. They snapped a rubber band at it. It moved and bumped a golf ball that rolled.

Carrie and Allison used two batteries that made a flashlight bulb glow. The light made a shadow happen on the other side of a walnut — for a little while.

Todd and Gina's mousetrap snapped shut. It turned a paddle. The paddle made a wheel turn.

"Excellent," Mr. Holliday said here, and "Now, *that's* what I call thinking," there.

"Good-looking flagman," he said when he came to David and Jilly.

"David made him," said Jilly.

"Jilly painted him," said David.

"Teamwork in action," said Mr. Holliday.

"We figured out a way to make our project sort of work with Ollie's and Erin's," said David.

"When did you do that?" asked Miss Kraft. "You should have cleared it with me."

"Just a little while ago," said David.

"You were busy helping Kevin," said Jilly.

"Ready?" said David. "Set — "

"Go!" Jilly pulled a string fastened to the flagman. The flagman's arm lifted, and the car began to roll. It went down the ramp and hit the first domino in a line of dominoes. One by one the long row of dominoes tipped over, clicking. The last one bumped a green-and-gold aggie. The marble rolled into a toilet paper tube and dropped into a can filled with marbles.

"Here's Erin's and my part," said Ollie. He tugged a string fastened to a cork. The cork popped out of a hole in the tin can. Marbles rattled out of the can, dropping down into a bowl full of water. As the bowl filled with marbles, the water spilled over and into a flat pan holding a small sailboat. The water rose, and the boat floated.

73

"Now's the best part," said Erin. She and Ollie leaned over the boat, blowing like crazy. The boat moved — until they had to stop blowing and giggle.

Ollie *could* laugh! He really could!

"Ready?" called Elvis. "Here we go for the big last act."

One by one, Peanut lifted books off the stack that held the balloon strings. Up rose the balloons — all but the Porcupine Balloon.

MOOOO-OOOOO-OOOO came the soulful cow sound as one of the dangling strings tipped over the moo-toy.

Tinggg! went the crystal bell as it rose swinging. *Tinggg. Tinggg.*

A draft from one of the windows carried the balloons overhead, tinging, toward a corner of the room.

"Porcupine Balloon!" shouted Elvis. "Here it comes." He moved the last book. The pin-covered balloon rose and was carried by the draft toward the others. It nudged them.

Pow! Bang! Pop! The balloons exploded as the Porcupine Balloon bumped into them.

Tinggg rang the crystal bell. *Tinggg* . . . *tinggg* and — *crash* as it dropped to the floor, shattering.

Peanut ran to look down at the bits of glass. "Oh, my gosh! I never thought that this would happen when I told Elvis it would be okay to pop all the balloons."

Jilly joined her. "Oh, pickle juice!" she said in awe, looking down at the billion bits of glass underfoot. "What's Ceci going to say?"

"Oh, Polly," said Miss Kraft. "I thought you were only going to break some of the balloons, not all of them. Why didn't you tell me you changed your mind? I'd have warned you."

"There goes my allowance for the rest of my life," moaned Peanut. "I'll have to buy another bell for Ceci. Only I can't get one from the Dells!" Things looked worse and worse. "No more Thirty-one Flavors, either. I think I'm going to die."

Jilly put her arm around Peanut.

"You'll have at least one ice-cream cone," said Mr. Holliday. He waved a handful of slips. "I'm leaving these Thirty-one Flavors gift certificates with Miss Kraft. It's my way of saying thank you to all of you. You have done a splendid job."

Everybody looked pleased and proud.

"You proved the point of our project," said Mr. Holliday, "and that is that KIDS CAN THINK!"

Miss Kraft walked to the door with him and stood there talking.

"Hey, Peanut."

Peanut turned.

Elvis was standing beside her. "I'll help pay for the new bell," he said. "This was half my fault." He didn't laugh or giggle or make a joke. He really meant it!

Four ladybugs, Peanut thought. Elvis got four ladybugs for niceness. But she didn't say that out loud.

CHAPTER
9

■▼■▼■▼■▼■▼■▼■▼■▼■▼■▼■▼■

They had lost recess time. But that was okay —
the make-happen project had been so much
fun. Now it was nearly time for art class.

"Boys," said Miss Kraft, "I want you to go
on down to the art room without me. Tell Mr.
Fortunato that the girls and I will be along in
a little while."

The boys went, with only a few words from
Ollie. "Is there something us guys ought to
know? What's going on?"

"Nothing overwhelming, Oliver," said Miss
Kraft. "Just girl stuff — you know, about hair
ribbons and pink nail polish. Things like that."

77

"Ugh," said Ollie.

"Go straight downstairs now," Miss Kraft called after the boys. "Kevin, please close the door."

She sat down on one of the desks at the front of the room. "Come close," she said, nodding at the desks around her.

The girls slid into the empty seats. Peanut and Jilly crowded into one desk and sat jammed together. At this moment, that was comforting.

"Girl stuff?" Peanut whispered in Jilly's ear.

"I've got this funny feeling something's going to happen," Jilly whispered back, "and I'm not going to like it."

Miss Kraft looked into the girls' eyes, each in turn. "Something was going on this morning," she said at last. "I haven't got the whole picture, but I know it made some of you feel bad. Want to talk about it?"

Nobody wanted to. Nobody spoke.

"Sometimes when bad things happen it helps to talk to a grown-up," said Miss Kraft. "I remember when I was about your age, a girl gave invitations to her birthday party to some of the girls in my class and not to others. The girls who didn't get invited were so unhappy."

Silence.

"Did you get an invitation?" Beth asked after a long moment.

Miss Kraft stared off into the distance, a remembering look in her eyes. "No. I felt utterly miserable. I cried."

Miss Kraft, of all people, hadn't gotten an invitation? Miss Kraft had cried?

"What happened?" asked Elena. "Did some grown-up make that girl invite the rest of you to her party?"

Miss Kraft shook her head. "Think," she said. "Would you want to go to a party if somebody was forced to ask you?"

We-e-e-ll . . . If you wanted to go to the party bad enough. . . .

Then, no, they decided. No. They would not go.

"I'd feel horrible inside if I did that," said Carrie. "Like I wasn't worth very much."

"Exactly." Miss Kraft nodded. "Your good feeling about yourself would suffer."

"But what did you *do*?" whispered Gina.

"My mother had a friend I liked a lot. She

used to take me places I enjoyed, like the museum and the ballet. I told her all about it. Somehow or other, I came to understand that some things are just like that. I got to feeling better about it. I don't know why, but I did. It helps to share things."

Again there was silence.

In the silence there was a hiccup. A shaky in-drawn breath followed. Elena's tears spilled over again. "I'm n-never," she sobbed, "going to be a popular person. M-My clothes aren't pretty. They're different."

A tumble of talk followed. Glasses . . . noses . . . crooked teeth . . . the ladybug test . . . skinny . . . fat . . . freckles . . . the ladybug test . . . the ladybug test . . .

Miss Kraft listened without speaking.

At last the talk slowed and died. Nobody had anything more to say.

"I know you don't always think so now," Miss Kraft said after a while. Her voice was soft. "But each of you is pretty in your own special way. And you will get even prettier as you enter your teens. We tend to grow into our noses and chins. Freckles get to be a kind of special individual beauty style. Sometimes teeth get straightened. But believe it or not, I can think of a movie star who is more interesting because her teeth are *not* perfectly straight. One star even has a famous collection of — freckles!

"But now" — she paused and looked around — "I want to hear more about this ladybug test."

All eyes turned toward Peanut and Jilly.

Slowly, taking turns, they explained. Not about giving the ladybug test to Miss Kraft, of course, but how the test worked and how it was going to let them know whether they would be popular when they grew up.

"Emmy and Erin gave the test to Jilly and me," said Peanut.

"We gave it to them," said Jilly.

"And we all got lots of ladybugs and hardly any spiders."

"We never thought that everybody would not get lots of ladybugs."

Peanut was feeling more awful by the moment — as though she were worth about a thousand spiders.

"It was so much fun," said Jilly. But this particular minute was no fun at all. Right now she felt as bad as she had the day she broke her mother's great-grandmother's sugar bowl.

"Whewwwww!" Miss Kraft let out a long breath. "Talk about cause and effect! But who'd think that an innocent game could make so many different kinds of people so unhappy in so many ways?"

Yes! Who?

If only, thought Peanut, we had planned ahead more. But — could they have guessed what would happen?

This is kind of like our make-happen projects, thought Jilly. Only we didn't mean to make everyone sad.

"You know," Miss Kraft went on, "as I see it, counting ladybugs isn't a half-bad idea."

"It isn't?" Peanut and Jilly said together.

Miss Kraft shook her head. "It's kind of fun, really. Where you went wrong was, you looked at each other with your own eyes, with your own values. You didn't look at each other as though you were that person. What one person thinks is pretty, or fun, or whatever, may not be the way another person sees things. None of us can know what it's like to be inside somebody else's skin."

True! Sometimes Jilly wondered and wondered what it would be like to be Peanut. And Peanut could never imagine what it would be like to be Jilly.

"If each of you had rated yourself, you'd have a better idea of your personal ladybug score. And there's something else to think about here, too," Miss Kraft went on. "About being popular . . .

"We're all supposed to be nice to each other — that goes without saying. But when people *try* to be popular, doing things just to make people like them — " She paused. She seemed to be thinking about how to say something so they would understand. "When people do that, they lose themselves."

The girls exchanged puzzled glances. How could you lose yourself?

"People who do that never become quite the people they could be. And strangely, they are never quite as popular as they would like to be. Popularity sort of collects around people who are uniquely themselves."

The room was still. Everybody was listening very hard.

"Now, I have an idea," said Miss Kraft. "Over the weekend, I want each of you to think of seven good things about yourself. Seven. Write them down. And I want each of you to decide how many ladybugs each one of those good things is worth. Forget the spiders. I cannot stand spiders." She shivered, and everyone laughed.

"Wouldn't it be terrible to be a spider instead of a girl?" asked Carrie.

Ick! Awful! Creepy! Yuck!

"When you come to school on Monday," said Miss Kraft, "bring your ladybug lists of special good things. I will go over your lists with each of you. Okay?"

Okay! Maybe the ladybug test was going to turn out to be fun after all. Everybody had begun to smile.

Miss Kraft stood up. "Let's go downstairs before Mr. Fortunato comes looking for us." She paused, a finger at her cheek. "Should I or shouldn't I?" she murmured to herself, looking around at the girls.

Should she what? Miss Kraft never needed help making up her mind. But if she did —

"Sure you should!" Peanut said positively.

Miss Kraft laughed. "Okay. I should. I'm just too happy to keep it to myself. I'll tell you a secret. You have just met my future husband."

"Husband?" squealed Peanut. She felt, suddenly, like one of Elvis's balloons, soaring up into the air.

"You are going to marry Mr. Holliday?" Jilly said in awe. Gone was the broken-antique-sugar-bowl feeling. She felt the way she did every time she came to the end of the Cinderella story.

"Pretty soon?" asked Carrie. "Are you going to be married soon?"

"Can we come to your wedding?" asked Emmy.

"Will you wear a veil?" "Will you have lots

of bridesmaids?" "And a flower girl?" Questions filled the air.

Miss Kraft was laughing. And so was Erin, her head thrown back, her mouth open wide. She looked just like Miss Kraft!

"I'm glad you're happy for me," said Miss Kraft as the girls crowded around her. "We won't be married until Mr. Holliday gets his doctorate — finishes at the university, that is. I'll tell you when we set the date. Now come. Let's go. Go, go, go!" She clapped her hands.

"Know something?" Peanut whispered to Jilly as they all trooped downstairs to the art room. "Maybe the ladybug test was right about Miss Kraft."

"I think so, too," Jilly whispered back. "All those ladybugs — they must have meant something."

As the rest of the girls pushed past them into the art room, Peanut and Jilly hung back.

"Know something else?" said Jilly. "We've got to apologize to Ollie. I guess we really weren't fair, not telling him."

Peanut groaned. "You know he's going to call us chuckleheads, muttonheads, airheads, and whatever other heads he can think of." She sighed. "But you're right. Let's get it over with."

They straightened their shoulders and went into the art room side by side. They could face anything — even Ollie — together.